MIRA DAY

To Josh.
I love you.

PROLOGUE
Brandon

1997- Age 5

"Mommyyy!"

Light is coming in my room from the hallway. Hugging my teddy bear, I wait for Mommy to come in. I'm thirsty and want some apple juice.

After a long time, I open my mouth to call for her again, but I stop. I hear Daddy, he's home from work and he's making a lot of noise from the kitchen. Hugging my teddy tighter, I climb out of bed and peek into the hallway.

"Mommy?" I try to be a little quieter now that Daddy's home. He scares me.

Sneaking into the kitchen, my Mickey Mouse

pajamas covering my feet, I peek around the corner. "Mommy?"

"What is it, Brandon?" Daddy's voice is low and grumble-y. He sounds tired but mad.

He's sitting at the table, holding his favorite cup – the one he puts his grown-up juice in. A bottle of his juice is next to him on the table. I know better than to bother Daddy when he has his juice.

"Um. I'm thirsty."

Daddy doesn't move.

"Where's Mommy?"

He pours more of his juice in his cup. "You tell me." His voice is scary now, like a monster.

I hear the front door open and Mommy comes around the corner. Her eyes go wide when she sees Daddy sitting at the table. "Johnny? What are you doing home, sweetie?" She looks at me. "And why are you out of bed?"

"I'm thirsty."

She wipes her hands on her skirt before picking me up. "You can have some water and then back to bed."

"But I want juice!"

"Where were you?" I look over my shoulder at Daddy.

They're going to fight again.

Mommy sets me on the counter, her hands holding my face for a second. Her smile small, but it's just for me. "At Jackie's."

I hear Daddy's chair scratch against the floor. "The

hell you were! Where were you?" I jump when his hand hits the table.

Mommy hands me my dinosaur cup and kisses my forehead. "Go back to bed, baby. I'll come tuck you in in a few." She hugs me before putting me on the floor. I take a drink and head back to my room.

"Don't yell while Brandon's in here." I hear her whisper.

Stopping in the hallway, I turn back. Curious, I glance into the kitchen.

Daddy is standing right in front of Mommy. "You were with that asshole down the street, weren't you?"

Mommy crosses her arms and glares up at him. "Jesus. Not this again, Johnny."

"I see the way you look at him."

"You're drunk." She pushes past him and he grabs her arms, spinning her to face him. His eyes narrow. "Tell me you've never touched him."

I see Mommy's mouth drop open a little bit. Daddy starts to shake her.

"You fucking whore!"

Scared, I run back to my room, jumping into my bed, and covering my head with my pillow. I can still hear them.

"Don't you fucking call me that!" I hear a loud smack.

"Oh, so you're gonna hit me now? Why shouldn't I call you that? It's what whores do. They go off, leaving their kids alone at home while they fuck the neighborhood."

"Let go of me!"

"You're a terrible mother and trash for a wife."

"Let go! You don't know what you're talking about!"

"Get out of my house!"

I hear her shoes drag across the floor before a door opens and slams shut. I hear loud banging on the door.

"Johnny! Let me back in!"

Mommy is yelling really loud.

Daddy's footsteps are heavy as they come down the hallway. I'm still in my bed, covering my head with the blanket. I squeeze my eyes shut, trying to block out the yelling outside.

Daddy pushes my bedroom door closed, and I feel him sit on my bed. His hand touches my leg as he pulls off my blanket. "Just me and you, kid."

I look at him while I listen to Mommy still banging on the house. Daddy takes a drink from his juice bottle. His face is sad.

"Let me in!"

"Go away, whore!" Daddy takes another drink.

"Please, Johnny! Don't do this."

Daddy stands up and slams my bedroom door into the wall as he walks into the hallway. I hear him throw open the front door and then more yelling.

Sitting up in bed, I watch out the window.

Daddy has Mommy by the arm again, and he's dragging her down the street. I watch as porch lights come on, one by one. Daddy stops a few houses down and pulls Mommy across the yard to the front door. After a moment, a man answers the door. Daddy pushes Mommy at the man and leaves, throwing his bottle on the ground.

A rain drop falls on my window and I watch as it slides down, followed quickly by more. I see Mommy run after Daddy while the man at the house stays by his door. I hear a squealing noise from a car coming down the street. Its lights pass over Mommy just before she hits the front window. I scream for her and hit my bedroom window.

Dropping my teddy bear, I run out of my room.

The rain is making the grass slippery, and I'm going to be in trouble for being outside in the rain. But I don't care. I'm running to get to Mommy.

I hear screaming and shouting, then a pair of arms scoop me up before I reach the end of the driveway. A flash of yellow hair is hiding my Mommy from me.

"Ssh, Brandon. Ssh." Jenny's mommy, Miss Jackie, is carrying me away, stroking my hair.

"Mommy!" I kick and struggle to be let down. "Mommy!" Choking, I let out a howl as she continues to walk away from the crowd growing in the street. To her house next door, not mine.

"I know, baby, I know." Miss Jackie holds me tighter as the rain falls harder.

Hush now, Brandon. Go to sleep.

"But... Mommy..." My head falls onto her shoulder and everything goes dark.

Daddy's hand is scratchy as he touches my cheek. He

bends over and whispers, "Don't cry. We won't have to worry about her leaving us anymore." His breath is stinky with spice and medicine and he is really sloppy with his words. I saw him drink something from a silver thing before the preacher started talking.

He drinks a lot of that stuff.

I sniff and continue to stare at the brown box surrounded with flowers.

Miss Jackie said Mommy went to Heaven. She told me it was a pretty place where she'll always be happy.

I want to go with Mommy, but no one will let me.

Daddy has been mad ever since Mommy was hit by the car. He keeps yelling, telling me that I'm bad and that it was my fault. They were happy before me.

He whispers to himself, asking why she's gone before getting angry again. I hear him when he looks at her picture, telling her he loves her before calling her a mean name.

A loud squeak scares me as the box in front of me falls into a hole in the ground. My hands reach out and I make a step toward it.

Before I can move, I feel someone behind me, hugging me tightly.

It's Jenny, my friend, from next door.

I drop my hands and stare at the ground. Tears fall onto my shoes. They're Spiderman shoes. Mommy got them for me. She told me they would make me strong and brave, like a superhero.

But I don't feel like Spiderman today. I feel... nothing.

Scared.

Lonely.

Sad.

Don't worry, Brandon. I'll take care of you.

I hear a voice I've never heard before; a man's voice. But when I turn, I only see Miss Jackie sitting on the ground next to me. There's no man around except Daddy and he's on the other side of the box.

Miss Jackie pulls me into her lap, hugging me, humming and rocking.

"Everything will be alright, baby."

CHAPTER ONE
Brandon

Present Day – Age 25

have always loved Fridays. Walking along Fremont Street in downtown Las Vegas with Jenny is something that keeps my heart beating. I watch the lights of the casinos dance in her eyes as she 'oohs' and 'ahs', knowing she's seen these lights a million times and it still excites her. It's just one more reason I love her.

We walk down the street laughing at the hordes of tourists taking it all in.

"You know you're just like them, right?" I point out as she squeals over some funny sign. "A local tourist."

"Shut up!" She laughs, her tongue darting out at me before getting sidetracked by a street performer.

As we make our way through the crowd, I slowly slip

my hand into hers, breathing a sigh of relief that she doesn't pull away. It's a familiar feeling, her hand in mine. But tonight, there's an electricity in the air.

She pushes her way through the people, trying to get to the darkened streets ahead of us while animatedly talking about her job at some local diner. I listen as her free hand waves widely as she speaks. I smile and nod, like I should, even though I can't hear a word she's saying. My heart is too busy thundering in my ears.

Just outside the Fremont Street Experience stands one of our favorite local bars, Atomic Liquors. A quieter spot in comparison to the glitz and glam of the Experience, but a legend that still attracts the tourists brave enough to step away from the lights. The Experience was fun when we were sixteen and looking for something free to do on a Friday night. At 21, we realized the real fun we could have just past the lights.

Most girls would probably be afraid of these streets, but not my Jenny.

She continues to prat on as we reach the outskirts while my brain kicks into overdrive. Tonight is the night. It has to be. It's our only time together anymore.

Our ritual for the past eight years broke when she went to college. Now that she's back, her time is taken up by work and her new boyfriend.

It's the only night of the week I feel... sane.

"Brandon, what are you staring at?"

I don't even realize I stopped walking. Jenny is looking back at me, one hand on her hip, the other still outstretched in mine, a fake annoyance playing on her pouty lips.

"Er, nothing." I pull my hand away from her grasp and stuff both of them into my pockets, brushing past her. Being so much taller than she is, she has to jog to catch up.

"Hey. You okay?" She places her hand on my arm and it's all I can do not to take that arm and wrap it around her. The wind blows her long strawberry blonde hair around her face, and I catch a whiff of her perfume. It's intoxicating. I don't think I can hold my tongue anymore. I want her. I need her and I need her to know tonight. The concerned look she has for me gives me the strength I need.

I swallow hard and put on my best smile. I can feel my lip quivering from nerves, and I want to punch myself for being such a pussy. Moving her hair away from her face, I tuck it behind her ear, allowing my hand to linger on her cheek, enjoying the warmth I can only get from her.

I smile and her gaze softens.

"It's nothing. Let's get that drink." I turn and open the door to Atomic. Jenny's eyes narrow, she clicks her tongue and walks past me. God, how does she make a pair of jeans so sexy?

We take our normal seats at the end of the bar as Andy, our bartender, places our usual beers down in front of us. Jenny leans over and gives Andy a hug as I give him a small nod of the head. He returns it before walking back to the other end.

A burley guy with a beard that won't quit, Andy's

been serving me for years. When Jenny left for school, he helped me get through it; one beer at a time. He even got a job as a bar back at a shithole closer to my house.

"So, how did your date go the other night?" She takes a swig of beer and turns to look me in the eyes. Her baby blues are bright against the dark bar background, the neon lights enhancing everything.

I shrug. "Meh. She was a bit boring."

"Jesus, I swear. If it's not one thing it's another." Jenny kicks my bar stool, laughing. I love it when she laughs. Her whole chest heaves and it's hard not to pay attention to that. "So what made her so boring?"

I lock my eyes on hers and take a pull from my beer. *She's not you.*

Swallowing, I lick my lips. "I don't know. She just didn't keep my interest."

"You still slept with her though, didn't you?"

Is that a glimmer of disappointment I see? Damn it, why does she have to know me well enough to know that?

I give her a sly smile and she punches me in the arm. "You dog! Sounds like she kept your interest peaked just long enough."

"Well, with tits the size of melons," I hold my hands out, "it's hard not to be a little interested." I instantly hate myself for saying that to her.

Way to go, Genius. Right before you confess your undying love to a girl, tell her about the sex you just had the other night. Smooth.

Luckily, my Jenny knows me. She gives me a scoff

before taking another drink. I focus on her lips wrapped around the bottle. The way her throat moves as the liquid makes its way down. My dick twitches, and I shift in my seat to ease the sudden confines of my pants. Jesus, what she does to me.

"Jenny, I need-"

I hear her phone ring, and she holds her hand up. "Hold that thought, B. Hello?" She starts to slide off the stool. "Hey sweetie! Let me go outside." She beams at me as she leaves.

I place my head in my hands, gripping my hair. Someone sets a shot in front of me, and Andy's gravelly voice breaks into my thoughts. "You alright?"

"Fuck." I slam the shot down and motion for another. "No dude. I'm not."

Andy sets the next shot down and leans against the bar. "You need to man up. Quit being a bitch." He raises his eyebrow as he pushes off, smirking.

"Pfft."

Smug asshole.

"Sorry!" Jenny gives me her breathy apology as she climbs back on her stool beside me. Her hand touches my back to brace herself, ander leg brushing against mine. Her touch sets my body on fire, as my eyes drawn to the hint of cleavage she's showing.

"That was Ronnie. He's stopping by."

I stare into the second shot glass. "Fuck Ronnie."

I want to immediately regret my words. I want to take them back and do this differently. But I don't. I don't regret saying what I said. Out of the corner of my eye, I watch her reaction.

"What the hell, Brandon?" She narrows her eyes. "I thought you liked Ronnie."

What is wrong with me?

"I can't do this anymore, Jenny." I don't even recognize my voice. It's deeper, with a touch of anger that I wish I could hide. I pour the second shot of bourbon down my throat, enjoying the burn.

"Do what?"

I inhale deeply. It's now or never. "Jenny. I love you."

Her brows furrow together. "I love you too, Brandon."

"No." I drink from my beer, my hands starting to shake. I set the bottle down. "Like, I'm *in* love with you."

I finally find the nerve to look at her. The understanding slowly registers on her face. Her mouth falls into a little 'O' as she turns back to face the bar.

The silence is suffocating.

"Brandon." Her voice is shaky and barely a whisper. "Don't."

I let out a long, slow breath.

Don't.

That's all she can say? My vision slowly starts to blur and a rage I haven't experienced since my dad died begins to surface. Before I can control it, I slam my hand onto the bar.

"Damn it Jenny." I growl. "Why not?! We're perfect together, and you fucking know it."

Stop cussing! You're going to scare her.

Who cares? She doesn't love you.

A tear falls from her face, and she quickly wipes it away. "You know I love you..."

"But just not enough." I finish off my beer and flag Andy down for another. He shakes his head slowly, pissing me off even more.

"It's not like that." She finally looks at me, her lips pursed in a pout as tears fall onto her cheek. A small part of me dies. "You've been my best friend all my life. I just... I just don't see you that way."

She might as well stab me in the heart.

"But you'll give that prick, Ronnie, a chance?"

"What has Ronnie ever done to you?"

"Other than fucking the woman I love?" I turn completely to face her. "You know it's just a matter of time before he leaves you anyway."

"What the-."

I shrug. "He's rich. You still live with your mommy. How much longer is he going to slum it with you?"

Anger flashes across her face as her hand makes contact with my cheek. "You're such an asshole."

She throws some money on the bar before turning to leave. The bar door closes abruptly behind her and all the anger I was feeling disappears. In its place, remorse.

"Shit!" Knocking my stool back, I chase after her.

Outside, she's walking down the street. "Jenny!"

In five steps, I'm right behind her, twirling her around to face me.

"Let go of me!"

I ignore her and pull her into my chest. She doesn't fight me as I hold her close, allowing her to cry into my jacket. "I'm so sorry."

"Jenny?" A red car pulls up beside us, and I see Ronnie in the passenger side window.

She steps back and wipes her eyes. "I need to go. I'll talk to you later." She gives me a faint smile before climbing into Ronnie's car while his eyes glare at me through the glass. I watch the rear lights fade down the road, my anger returning.

She's just going to leave it like that huh?

I let out a frustrated yell before walking back into the bar. Andy is wiping down the area Jenny and I were just sitting.

"I need a beer." I pick up my stool and fall onto it. I lean into my hands, pressing my palms into my eyes.

"Nah, dude. You're cut off."

My head jerks up. "What?"

Andy stops cleaning. "You're pissed, man. I get it. But you were just losing it in here. Beer ain't gonna help." He points a thick finger at me. "You need to calm down. She's a good girl and you fucked up." He crosses his arms over his chest. "Own it."

The lights seem to fade as I stand up. "Fuck you, man." My voice is deeper again as I slam the stool into the bar. Turning on my heel, I leave.

A few rare raindrops hit the pavement as I watch the lights still dancing in the distance. The same lights I was just under with Jenny.

It's raining. Just like when mom died...

Shoving my hands deep in my pockets, I walk back to the lights of downtown Vegas.

I did blow it.

And now I need something to blow off some steam, and I know just the strip club that will do the trick.

CHAPTER TWO
Brandon

"Dude!" Michael leans back in his seat, reaching out to shake my hand as I sit next to him. The strip club is pretty empty, but I knew I'd find him here. He flags the waitress for a drink as I start to relax into the chair.

Michael lived in the house Jenny moved into. He was my best friend as a kid before he moved away. I ran into him at a rival football game freshman year of high school. Turns out, his family moved to a neighboring city, not across the country. But as five year olds, how were we to know the difference?

I remember Jenny trying so hard to be a part of the high school experience. Pep rallies, homecoming, and all that shit. Me? I was happiest under the bleachers with a pack of cigarettes. Michael had the same thoughts I did that night. Said his parents figured it'd be good for him to go to the game and dropped him off. I stayed under the crowd until the game ended, Jenny in the stands with her mom.

"Hey man. What's up?"

Michael shrugs, holding his hands up in the air. "Just enjoying the scenery." He flicks a bill onto the stage, winking at the girl on the pole. He turns to me. "Things didn't go well with Jenny I see?"

I knead my eyebrows together as the waitress sets a PBR can in front of me. Michael's drink of choice. I'd much rather lick an ashtray, but it's cheap and it'll do the trick. "How did you know?"

"'Cause it's Friday. You're always out with her on Fridays." He sits up dramatically, grabbing my jacket sleeve. "That prick cock blocked you, didn't he?"

"You could say that." I roll my arm away from Michael's grasp and take a drink from the can, trying not to taste it as it goes down. I stare at the ground, thinking. "No. I fucked it up. I started cussing and... yelling." My head falls into my hands. "I'm pretty sure I called her slum, er, something like that." I grunt. "What the hell?"

Michael's arm falls onto my shoulder. "Don't beat yourself up so much, B. I'm sure she'll come around." I look up at him. "She may even give you some of that sympathy sex." He winks and guffaws as he chugs the rest of his beer.

"You're such a dick."

"And don't you wish you could be like me?" Michael

flags for another beer, grabbing another cocktail waitress that passes by. She smirks before rolling her eyes at his lame attempts at getting a free lap dance.

Michael's question wasn't a question. It was a statement. He knows I want to be more like him. Laid back. Unnerved by nothing. I take another swig.

Michael didn't lose his parents.

Michael didn't lose the love of his life to another guy. A better guy, at that.

Michael has his strippers and PBR and he was content.

I finish the can and crush it in my hand. Michael whoops, finishing his new beer. "That's what I'm talkin' about!" He beckons the girl coming off the stage to us, pulling her into his lap. "Time to get crazy!" He pats my knee. "Trust me, bro. She'll come around."

I nod as another girl straddles me, and I give in to the night.

CHAPTER THREE
Jenny

 onnie is snoring beside me, his arm haphazardly draped over my stomach. I reach out to the night stand for my phone.

3:34 am.

I'm exhausted, my eyes burning as they fight sleep. But I can't. Every time I close them, all I can see is Brandon.

The guilt of rejecting him like I did is eating at me. And lying beside another guy isn't helping.

Finally giving in, I shift out from under Ronnie's arm and stand to get dressed.

As I'm buttoning my pants, Ronnie shifts, waking up. "Babe? What are you doin'?"

I lean onto the bed and kiss his cheek. "I'm going

home. I can't sleep."

He yawns. "What time is it?"

"3:45."

He turns on his lamp, blinking. "Why can't you sleep?"

I shuffle, looking at my feet. "I feel bad for fighting with Brandon."

Ronnie rubs his face, sighing. "Jenny, he's a big boy. He'll get over it."

I sit next to him on the bed. "No. You don't get it." Biting my lip, I think of how to explain this. "Brandon hasn't really been the same since his dad died. He's been – bitter. Angry. I'm worried about him."

"Sweetie, how long has it been? Two, three years? He needs to move on." My jaw drops. Ronnie raises his hand to stop me. "I'm sorry. But he needs to pull it together." He takes my hand. "You can't keep taking care of him. I know you want to, but he's an adult. Stop babying him."

"I know. You just don't understand how he grew up." I quickly wipe a small tear away. "He had it rough. Too rough. My mom and I are all he has."

Ronnie gives me a pointed look. "So you've said." He takes a deep breath before giving me a forced smile, his hand at my cheek. "You have a big heart, Jenny. But is it big enough to love two guys?"

My mouth falls open. "But it's not like that! I don't want-."

He presses his finger to my lips. "Ssh. I know, baby. I

didn't mean to insinuate that you love him like you love me."

I pull my hands away from him, crossing my arms tightly across my chest. "Yes you did."

Ronnie's hands grip my wrists, pulling them apart. "Can you blame me?" My face flushes as he continues. "Jenny, why do you think I moved to Vegas? Huh?" He tilts my chin to look at him. "I love you and I'm ready for us to begin a life together. But how can we do that if Brandon keeps this up?"

I feel my lip quiver as I search the room for some answer.

He's right. Brandon needs to understand that we're friends. That I'm with Ronnie, not him.

"You're right." My voice is small. "This isn't fair to us. I'm sorry."

Ronnie kisses my cheek. "Don't be sorry, sweetie. You're a caring person. I love that about you."

I smile, wiping more tears from my cheeks.

He steals a quick kiss on my lips before settling back onto his pillows. "Now, are you sure you want to leave?" He draws back the sheets next to him. "I know something that might take your mind off your troubles..." He wags his eyebrows before giving me an exaggerated wink.

Giggling, I smack his arm. "Go back to bed. I'll call you later." Kissing him again, I leave.

The streets are quiet as I drive from Summerlin to North Las Vegas. The emptiness surrounding me doesn't help my guilt.

As I weave my way toward my neighborhood, my thoughts drift to Brandon. He looked so sad as Ronnie drove away. How long has this been going on? How did I not see?

Brandon has been my best friend since I saw him standing on my front step, holding onto his GI Joe. His parents forced him to come meet me, but I knew we'd be close. At that age, I called him my boyfriend because that's what he was. A boy and a friend. I never understood why the adults would giggle when I made this declaration.

I lean my arm against the car window, laying my head against it. I remember when I started seeing Brandon as a possible boyfriend. It terrified me to think of seeing him as someone I might want to kiss. To marry. To go to prom with. Because back then, that was how I thought. It was the perfect story, a fairytale, of soulmates, growing up next to each other before hormones kicked in and made them realize they wanted something more.

But I watched him with other girls in school. While I kept my head down and deep into the books, he skipped class to fool around with only God knows who. I wanted college, it was never in his plans. We didn't have the same future in mind and so I never gave into those thoughts.

Plus, he was so sad. All the time. He hid it from almost everyone. Except me. He needed me to be there for him. Not as some horny chick, but as his best friend.

The orange glow of the street lights shine through my car, passing by like each memory I'm having.

I love Brandon. More than I should. But I need him to move on. If he wants me to be his friend, he needs to be Ronnie's friend too.

His hurtful words at the bar come to mind and I frown. I worry that even our love won't hold this friendship together.

I let out a forced breath and take a look at myself in the rearview mirror. "Ronnie's right. I'm babying him."

I watch my jaw clench, as the words tumble from my mouth. I glare at myself. "Sure Jenny, tell yourself some more lies."

Brandon needs someone. His past is too damaging to be left alone. For the past three years, I've watched him sink further into himself. He mutters, forgets things and his mood changes in an instant.

I frown; my head starting to hurt.

Maybe Mom will know what to do.

Turning into my driveway, I glance at Brandon's house next door. He's not home.

I look down the street, wondering why he's still out. A hint of nerves flutter through my stomach while I check my phone.

As if he knew, a text from Brandon pops onto the screen.

Brandon: *I'm sorry. P.S. Don't kick your flowers.*

I look to the front door to see a small bouquet on the

front stoop, the porch light shining like a spotlight. I smile, the knots slowly loosening in my stomach.

He's fine.

I pick up the flowers and unlock the door. Turning the corner into the kitchen, I find a vase and fill it with water.

We're fine.

CHAPTER FOUR
Jenny

2009 - Age 17

watch the paper flutter out of my locker as I open the door. Squatting down to pick it up, I notice the sloppy writing of a guy.

I grin as I open it, wondering who it's from.

"Hey."

I jump at the sound of Brandon's voice. I whirl around, my smile quickly disappearing, dropping the paper.

The bruise around his eye is deep purple and slightly swollen. It's the third one I've seen this month.

"Oh, Brandon." The words barely a whisper.

He waves his hand to dismiss it. "It's fine."

I glance around the hall. "No. It's not fine. What

happened?"

He gives me a hard look. "I told him to fuck off."

"Brandon. You have to tell someone."

He ducks his head. "No. Can you just help me hide it?" His face is flush. He notices the paper on the ground and picks it up. "What guy is drooling over you this week?"

I roll my eyes, turning to grab my makeup bag. "Shut up." I smirk. "That doesn't happen."

"My dearest Jenny." Brandon's eyebrows raise in amusement. He leans up against the lockers, holding the note out of my reach. "I think you're the most beautiful girl in school." His eyes travel down the paper, chuckling as he goes.

"Oh, I like the ending. 'I hope you like me and give me a chance. I think we'd have fun together.'" Brandon grimaces. "You know what that means." He makes an 'o' with one hand and puts his finger through it.

I smack his arm. "Ew, Brandon! Stop. That's gross."

He laughs, crumbling the paper. "I'm just sayin'. That's all these guys are after."

"Who's it from?"

"Why?" Brandon's eyes go wide. "You wanna lose it to this loser?" He holds what remains of the notebook paper up. "Dude couldn't even spell gorgeous."

I snatch the ball of paper from him. "No." I swallow. "I'm just curious." I stuff it into my backpack, shutting my locker door. "Come on. Let's get that covered."

We still have fifteen minutes before the first bell, and

31

kids are starting to fill up some vacant tables in the lunch room. I take his hand and drag him past their glances to an empty table in the outside foyer behind the cafeteria. Brandon's fingers tighten around mine, sending a wave of heat deep into my belly.

"Sit."

He does, facing away from the table, tilting his head up so I can apply some foundation. We're quiet for a while, no one outside with us.

"Is that what you're after?" I ask, finally breaking the silence.

"What?" Brandon's eyes are closed, his face softer than normal. I like that I can help him relax.

"Sex. You said that's what all guys are after."

Brandon's eyes open slightly. "I mean. I won't turn it away." He grins. I take notice of his mouth. He has a small cut along his top lip that's finally healing from three weeks ago. I swallow hard, my mouth dry.

Brandon's always been cute. His shaggy brown hair and deep brown eyes, along with a lanky build, completes his skater boy look.

Even if he's never even touched a skateboard.

The bruises make him look... what's the word? Dangerous? Girls seem to fawn over him, thinking he's just some bad boy, some guy they can play out their sick fantasies of fixing him. Little do they know his stories are all cover-ups. He plays the lies well, but they have no idea.

I guess I never really noticed the appeal.

Until now.

Normally, the idea of talking about sex with anyone outside of a classroom setting would make me blush. But a weak, curious part of me wants to know what he thinks.

"Is that why you talk to Candy Taylor?"

He blushes. "I never have to ask her for it."

I flinch. "Ugh, Brandon. You're disgusting."

He flashes me another grin. "Why do you ask, Jenny?" I feel his hands press lightly on the back of my knees. My eyes dart to the ground.

"No reason."

Brandon's staring at me now, his hands moving slowly up and down my legs.

I pull his head straight. "Close your eyes. I need to finish."

He swallows, his tongue darting out quickly. I mirror him and suddenly, I'm burning up.

Hormones.

The ringing of the 1st period bell startles me. I step back, trying to get some distance between me and him.

"I think that should do the trick."

Brandon grabs his backpack. "Thanks again, Jenny." He steps to me, wrapping his arms around my shoulders. My face is buried in his army green jacket, and I smell a mixture of cigarette smoke and Old Spice.

What is going on?

"Brandon?"

I pull away from his warmth and see Candy come into view. I look up at Brandon, his Cheshire cat smirk making me nauseous.

"Take it you're not coming to class?"

He shrugs, kissing my forehead. "We'll see." He winks and turns away, throwing his arm around Candy. She glances back smugly. Rolling my eyes, I grab my backpack and rush down the hall to class.

Brandon

I flick my cigarette to the ground, blowing out the last bit of smoke as I grind the butt with my heel. My head is killing me.

"Hey B! What's up?"

I turn around to see Michael walking up to me, his shit-eating grin contagious.

I reach for his hand pulling him into a quick hug. "Dude! What are you doing here?"

Michael shrugs. "Knew you'd be around. Figured cutting school is no fun solo."

I shake my head before I catch sight of *him*.

Dave Davenport.

I sneer, pulling another cigarette out of my pocket. I hold the pack out for Michael and he grabs one.

"Who's the douche?" He asks, flicking his lighter on, nodding his head in Dave's direction.

"Dave. He left Jenny a note in her locker." I twist my neck to loosen the knots.

"Wait. Your Jenny? Dude." Michael pulls a drag, blowing out the smoke with his last words. "Not cool. You need to end that."

I nod, catching Dave's eye. He continues toward the field, our gazes locked.

"That stupid jock is nowhere near good enough for our Jenny."

"Nowhere." I mutter, trying to drown out the blood pounding in my ears.

My headaches have been getting worse. Usually they happen around the time Dad starts knocking me around. I push my palms into my eyes, trying to focus, drowning out Michael's string of curses and insults.

I've never seen Jenny so flustered before. She's so cute when she blushes. And damn that bell. I was just about to kiss her. She wanted it. And not from some dumb jock or that rich prick from gym class but me, *me*. The dirt bag best friend; I turned her on. I caused that shiver I could feel in her knees. I caused that flush in her cheeks.

I'm glad Candy came when she did. Otherwise, today could have been rough. But like I said, I never have to beg with her.

The idea of Jenny and I together has plagued my mind for years. But even I'm not good enough for her. And definitely not Davenport. I take a drag of my cigarette and blow out some smoke.

I could be though.

"Are you listening, Brandon? Come on! Jenny's finally coming around, and this asshole is trying to get in her pants? Fuck that."

My vision darkens as my body seems to fall away, Michael's voice fading into the background.

"You know what? I got this. You just relax. He won't ask our Jenny out anymore."

Jenny

Reaching into my bag for 2nd period, my hand lands on the crumbled-up paper ball from earlier. I sneak a peek at the guys in the room, waiting to see if any of them look in my direction.

Slowly, I open the ball of paper and read it. Whoever wrote this has terrible grammar. Brandon was right to chuckle.

But his words are sweet and I rush through the rest to get to the name.

Dave Davenport.

My jaw drops as I read and reread the name.

Dave is one of the popular guys. The captain on the football team and a prom king if I ever saw one.

I fan my face, trying to tone the red down. Dave likes

me? There must be a mistake. Looking at his name, I let out a nervous giggle.

Nope, no joke. It's really there, in black and white.

Most of 2nd period is a blur as I think about what going on a real date with him will be like. I've never been on one. What do you wear? How do you act? I slump. I need more girlfriends to figure this out.

A knot forms in my stomach as the bell rings for 3rd period. What is Brandon going to say when I go? *If* I go?

Whatever it was that almost happened with Brandon this morning is still in the back of my mind, slowly creeping its way into the front.

I wanted to kiss him. My best friend. The guy who just three seconds before admitted to being the stereotypical, high school horn dog. I wanted to kiss *him*. And I'm pretty sure he wanted to kiss me.

But we didn't kiss. In fact, he walked off with Candy Taylor, without another look back at me.

I wander to my next class, replaying how I felt with Brandon this morning.

No.

Not Brandon.

I *can't*.

We've been together for years. I know more about him than anyone, including his own dad. Our relationship is so much more than a random kiss before class.

It's deeper.

Special.

He needs me, and not to date. That won't end well at

all.

No.

Plus, he has Candy.

And I have a first date to think about.

Brandon

My hands are trembling as they clutch the sink. I splash some cold water onto my face, wiping a smear of blood from my newly cut lip.

What. The. Hell?

This is usually how I find myself after an episode with dad, but at school? The last thing I remember is smoking under the bleachers with Michael.

Relax, Brandon. He won't bother her now. She won't leave us.

I stare at the mirror, frowning.

Dave Davenport likes Jenny.

How do I live up to him?

I splash more water on my face, giving up on trying to remember anything. I never can.

Grabbing a stack of paper towels, I dry up and grab my bag.

I don't live up to him. He can give Jenny nice things;

I can't. She'll go out with him and forget all about me.

Like Mom?

I shudder at the anger growling through my head.

"No. Not like mom."

She's just going to leave you like your whore mother did. Same thing.

My shoulders shrug, and I shake my head to clear it.

"It's not the same." I mutter, throwing open the door and stepping into the hallway.

Jenny

I'm already in my seat during my last class. The class I'm in with Dave. I shift nervously as my classmates start to file in, stealing glances at the door before returning my eyes to my desk.

What do I say to him?

Will he sit next to me?

Oh God, I hope I don't have anything in my teeth!

Brandon wasn't at lunch, but neither was Candy, so I'm sure he's skipped everything to be with her. Would have been nice to talk to him about this. I don't know many girls I would call friends, just Brandon. The few that may hang around are there more for Brandon. I guess I'll talk to Mom when I get home.

I see Dave come through the door, and I'm pretty sure I'm going to throw up. He sees me and stops. Narrowing his eyes, he walks toward my desk.

I put on my best shy smile and drop my eyes. Trying to be flirty, and probably failing, I look back up through my eyelashes. Dave grimaces before sitting down.

Two desks away from me.

Away from me.

He didn't even smile at me.

In fact, he looks pissed.

I grab my makeup mirror and check my hair; my makeup; my nose. Nothing wrong. Nothing out of place.

I take his note out of my book, reading it again.

It's signed by him.

It has my name on it.

What could be his problem?

Class barely holds my attention, and I just chalk this day up as a loss. I can't keep my eyes from the back of Dave's head.

I watch him as he wiggles, adjusts, scratches and stares at his desk.

Finally, he looks back at me. Catching my eye, he jerks back to look at the projector screen.

Tears prick my eyes. I'm such a fool. Of course Dave doesn't like me.

I use the last few minutes of class to focus on the projector, but I can't see through the few tears that have escaped. I don't know why I'm so upset. It's not like I really liked Dave or something.

As soon as the bell rings, I slam my notebook shut and angrily shove it into my bag. Whoever played this prank is a jerk. What did I do to be humiliated like this?

"Jenny?"

My head snaps up and I see Dave staring down at me. I didn't notice before, but he has a bruise forming on his cheek.

What the...

Dave rocks on his heels. "Listen, can we talk?"

My mouth goes dry as I nod. Standing up from my desk, I follow Dave outside the classroom and he turns abruptly. So abruptly that I run into him. He quickly backs up, leaving a lot of space between us.

"Jenny." He lets out a long sigh. "Why did you show Brandon my note?" He sounds angry, hurt even.

I kick the ground with my toe. "It was an accident. I dropped it." I pause. "Wait. How do you know that-"

"You know, I really liked you." He ducks his head. "But don't worry, Brandon made it pretty clear that we couldn't go out."

"What are you talking about?"

"Hey Jenny."

As if summoned, Brandon runs up behind me, his lip cut open again.

Dave takes a step back. "Look man. I'm not asking her out, okay?" He pulls on his backpack straps. "Don't need this." He puts his hands up in surrender, taking another step back.

I spin around. "Brandon! What did you do?"

Brandon's eyebrows furrow. "What are you going on about?" He looks up at Dave, backing down the hall. "Wait, what was he sayin'?"

I look back to Dave who's dropped his hands. "Jenny, you need to control your friend." He points at Brandon. "He's fucking crazy." Dave turns his back and continues down the hallway.

"Brandon," I hiss, "What happened to your lip? And Dave's cheek? Did you fight him?!"

His mouth falls open. Running a hand through his hair, he shakes his head. "No. I, I don't think so."

"You don't think so? No, Brandon. You either did or you didn't."

He shrugs. "No," he says, shaking his head. "No. Jenny, come on. This cut was from my dad, remember?" He glares down the hall at Dave's retreating back. "What did that asshole tell you?"

I throw my hands in the air. "Nothing! I thought he was going to ask me out, but instead, he tells me that you made it clear he wasn't to talk to me."

I push past Brandon, embarrassment washing over me for the millionth time today. I'm done. I just want to go home and curl up in front of the television. Today can burn in Hell.

I hear Brandon skid around me, stopping in front of me and holding onto my shoulders. "Jenny, listen, really. I have no idea what he's talking about." He tilts his head off to the side, another one of his smirks surfacing. "I'm really sorry, okay? For whatever it is that I did, I'm sorry." He places his finger under my chin, tugging my face softly to look at him.

I wipe my eyes. "I believe you." I jab a finger into his chest. "But let's be clear. You can't go around hitting guys just because they leave me a stupid note."

"Fair enough." Brandon smiles, wrapping his arms around me. "Come on. I know some ice cream that's calling your name." He kisses the top of my head and moves to the side so we can walk, his arm still draped over my shoulders. "My treat."

I take a final peek over my shoulder but Dave's not there.

Ice cream is a must tonight.

Jenny

randon?”

I tap on the screen door.

No answer.

Opening the door, it squeaks loudly, announcing my intrusion. “Hello?” I call out.

The screen door is attached to the kitchen, the living room around the corner. I can hear the television so I know he's home. I set a bottle of Jim Beam on his kitchen counter, along with my purse.

Peering around the corner, I don't see anyone in the living room.

“What are you doing here?”

Startled, I jump to see Brandon standing in the hallway. He's dressed in a pair of low hung jeans and nothing else. Worry comes over me as I notice his thin frame.

I push the need to make him some dinner away as I watch him. He seems to be swaying a bit and his eyes are heavy and glassy.

"The door was open."

He shrugs, walking into the kitchen. I follow, nervous butterflies fluttering into my throat.

He stops in front of the bottle of bourbon and plays with the yellow ribbon I tied around the neck. "What do you want, Jenny?"

He sounds like a gruffer version of himself. The voice makes my skin crawl. Never the less, I take his hand. He allows me, turning around, but with a guarded look.

"I just wanted to say thank you for the flowers. And that I'm sorry."

Releasing my hand, he crosses his arms across his chest, staring at his bare feet.

"Sorry for what?"

He's really not going to make this easy.

"For last night. For leaving before we could," my face starts to redden, "talk. About us."

The hurt displayed on his face makes my stomach flip. As much as I want to comfort him, I can't. I need to be strong. "Brandon, you have to understand that you mean the world to me."

His body slumps suddenly. "But that's not enough." His voice softens to one I recognize. Only it's discouraged and empty.

I bite my lip and slowly shake my head, fighting back tears. "I'm sorry."

Brandon turns away, his hands bracing the counter top. I wait.

"Remember when you would help me hide my bruises? That one morning, outside? You stood between my legs, my hands running up behind your knees..."

The blush of the memory tingles up my body, sending warmth into my cheeks. "That was a long time ago, Brandon."

Quickly, he straightens up, grabs the bottle of Beam and takes a swig. Slamming the bottle down, he turns back to me. His face is harder, almost angry. I swallow as he takes a step toward me.

Gripping my arms roughly, his breath heavy with alcohol, Brandon growls. "Don't you get it? You and Ronnie aren't going to last. You're wasting your time with him and the quicker you realize that we're meant to be together, the better we'll all be."

His lips are on mine before I can blink. They're wet and warm as they move against mine. I feel his tongue press against my lips, forcing itself into my mouth. I stand there, helpless with my arms pinned.

That day outside the cafeteria comes rushing back in full force. The feeling of wanting him washing over me – followed by the hurt and confusion I felt when he left with Candy. Leaving me alone.

I can feel his frustration, and he finally gives up. The urgency in his kiss slows down, and his hands loosen from around my arms.

Pulling away, he keeps his forehead to mine. "I just, needed to kiss you." His eyes drop. "For years. Longer than I can remember."

"I need to go."

His arms squeeze around me. "Please. Stay?"

I push him back gently, avoiding his eyes. "I need to go." I can barely raise my voice above a whisper. The despair coursing through my body is almost crippling.

How can we possibly go back to the way it was?

I push past him, grabbing my purse. "Can I talk to you later?"

Brandon nods, crossing his arms again.

Closing himself off from me.

Closing himself off from everything.

Without another word, I slip out of the house.

"What's going on with you, sweetie?"

Instantly, I feel guilty for slamming my mother's door. "Sorry, Mom. It's... Brandon. We had a fight."

She smiles faintly as she sits on the couch, patting the cushion next to her. I slump into the seat, exhaling loudly as I rub my face with my palms.

"So," Mom knits her hands together in her lap. "Brandon's in love with you."

I stop rubbing my face and turn to stare at her. "How do you know that?"

Mom waves her hand in the air with a smirk. "Oh, Jenny, that boy has been in love with you since forever.

Besides," she points at the dining room table. "That may be the most romantic arrangement of flowers I've ever seen."

I poke my head around her to see roses, baby's breath, and some light purple flower that I can't name.

It is gorgeous.

But not enough to forget his behavior.

I fall back into the couch. "Nosy much?"

Mom shrugs, picking at her pants. "My house."

I smirk. *This woman.*

"Well, he's going to have to do more than flowers."

"What happened?"

I turn to face her fully, my knees drawn up to my chest. "We went out, like we do every Friday. When we got to the bar, he drops this," I sputter, "bomb."

My mother chuckles. "And what did you say?"

I bite my lip. "I told him I love him too, but I don't see him like that." The emotions of last night start to surface. "He got really mad and…" My voice trails off.

Mom frowns.

I look at my hands. "He was going off about how a guy like Ronnie isn't going to stick around with a girl like me. And that I need to just be with him; save myself the heartache."

"A girl like you?"

I nod. "Be-because I still live at home and we're not, I don't know, rich." I shrug. My life with my mom has been wonderful. After her and Dad divorced, she moved us out to Nevada to start fresh. We never had much, and

Dad was no help. But she did everything she could for me. Thinking about what Brandon said has me fired up again. Screw his feelings.

Mom's frown deepens. "That doesn't sound like him."

"I know!" I throw my hands up. "He was being such an asshole. Mom, I slapped him before I stormed off. He chased me down, but I just needed to get away from him."

"What now?"

I grimace. "Ronnie says I baby him too much."

"And what do you think?" Mom asks.

"I feel terrible. Ronnie seems to be hinting that I'm going to leave him, which only makes me feel worse." I drop my head to knees. "But we're all he has. I worry about him."

"I know, sweetie. Me too. But you have to do what's right for you. If you see a future with Ronnie, it's not selfish for you to focus on that." She smiles. "Brandon may not like it, but he does love you. He's not going to stop being your friend."

I scoff. Mom pats my knee as she stands up, leaving me to my thoughts.

A few minutes go by before I follow her into the kitchen. I take my place next to her at the sink and help her clean some vegetables.

A small window over the sink looks out to the backyard, Brandon's house sitting on the left side. I can see him sitting in an old rocker on the back porch, his hand grasping a glass resting on his knee. He's staring off into the distance. The only movement is his foot, helping him to rock.

I grit my teeth and focus on peeling a potato. "I went to his house to talk to him about last night, but he's drunk. Probably shouldn't have brought him a bottle of Beam as an apology."

"I suppose not." Mom hands me a carrot. "He's heartbroken, Jenny. Men take rejection hard. Let him come to you when he's ready to talk."

I scowl as I watch him lift the glass to his lips.

Waiting around has never been my strong suit.

SIX
Brandon

1997 - Age 5

Brandon! Put the toys down and come on."

Mommy is using her mad voice, and her hands are on her hips.

Slowly, I drop one of my action figures and continue to sit, clutching my favorite GI Joe.

I don't wanna go.

I don't wanna meet the people living in Michael's house. I hate them. Michael wouldn't have moved away if they hadn't come.

"Brandon."

I let out a frustrated grunt. "I don't wanna!"

Mommy walks into my room and picks me up, my hand still wrapping around my GI Joe. "I don't care.

You're going."

I cry out, kicking my legs to get down but Mommy is holding me too tight to get anywhere.

Daddy is standing next to a tall table in the living room. It has bottles of brown water and fancy grown-up cups on it. He says that if he ever catches me near it, he'd whoop me.

Daddy means that.

He slams one of his cups down with a loud crash and I stop moving.

"Brandon. Behave or get the belt." His tone is scary, like a monster. Daddy wipes his mouth with his shirt sleeve. "Let's go."

Mommy puts me down, and we walk across the yard to the house next door. A van is in the driveway where Michael's mommy's car used to be.

We climb the front steps, and Daddy knocks on the door.

"I'll get it!"

I hear someone running to the door. It's thrown open by a girl with chocolate on her face.

"Hi!" She says behind the screen door before running away.

"Moooommmmyyyyy!"

"Jenny, please, don't make me regret that ice cream." A lady chuckles before opening the screen. "Hi. May I help you?"

Mommy reaches her hand out. "Hi. I'm Natalie. This is my husband, Johnny and our son, Brandon. We live next door."

"Nice to meet you." The lady shakes Mommy's hand. "I'm Jackie and this mess," she pulls the little girl from behind her legs, "is Jenny."

I stare at Jenny. She's a little shorter than me, with big blue eyes and yellow hair. Her dress has flowers on it. My face feels hot as I drop my head to stare at my shoes.

"Please, come in."

"Come on, Brandon." I feel Mommy push lightly on my back to walk into the house.

"Oh!" Mommy stops pushing me. "I forgot the cookies." She looks down at me. "Sweetie, will you be a big boy and run back to get them?"

I nod and start to climb down the steps.

"Me too?!" I turn around to see Jenny tugging at her mommy's dress.

"Okay but come right back."

Jenny follows me before skipping alongside me.

"I like dolls."

I scowl. "Dolls?"

She points to my hands. "That."

"It's a GI Joe, not a doll!" I stop in my tracks, my hands on my hips like Mommy. I want her to know I'm serious.

Jenny looks at my hands and back at me. "Looks like a dolly. We can play dollies together!" Her face seems to brighten.

"Gross! I'm not playing dolls with you. I'm a boy and we don't play dolls." I stomp my foot.

Jenny scrunches her face before shrugging. "Okay." She turns and walks up to my front door and opens it.

"Hey!" I run in after her. "That's my house!"

Bursting in, I look around but I don't see Jenny. I pad into the kitchen to find her dragging a chair away from the table.

"What are you doing?"

She ignores me as she moves the chair to the counter, huffing as she climbs it and sits on the counter. Reaching into the bowl Mommy has the cookies in, she grabs one and takes a bite.

My mommy made those.

Those are *my* cookies.

Looking at me, Jenny pats the counter with her hand. "Come here." She holds out her cookie. "Eat one with me."

My eyes dart to the front door before climbing onto the kitchen chair she used to get onto the counter. She reaches into the bowl and hands me one.

I take a bite as Jenny hums beside me, bouncing up and down. She looks like she's dancing.

"I like cookies!" She takes another bite, swinging her legs.

I watch her legs, kicking beside me. Slowly, I start to move my legs. I giggle. It feels like I'm running but I'm not.

"I like cookies too."

Jenny cheers, hugging my neck. "Let's be friends, okay?"

I look at her, thinking, before I nod. "Okay."

Her eyes get really big and she crawls off the counter. "Let's go play!" She runs out of the kitchen and crashes through my front door.

"Wait for me!"

Grabbing the bowl of cookies, and still hanging on to my GI Joe, I carefully climb down and chase after Jenny. She's not outside, and I know Mommy needs these cookies. I don't wanna get in trouble so I walk back to Jenny's house.

As I walk back in, I hear the grown-ups talking but no Jenny. I start to get scared. I hope she didn't run away.

"There you are! Brandon, give them to Miss Jackie." Mom smiles as I walk to Jenny's mommy.

"Here, Miss Jackie." I hand her the bowl, shuffling from one foot to the other.

"Thank you, Brandon. Jenny is in the backyard if you want to go play."

I stop moving, letting out a big breath. She's fine. "Okay." I run through the kitchen and out the back door.

Jenny is sitting in a sandbox with a shovel and pale. She has a doll sitting next to her as she lets sand fall from her shovel.

"Brandon, wanna build a sand castle?"

I plop down in the sand box, shaking my head. "I don't know how."

She starts moving the sand into a big pile. "It's easy. I'll show you."

I watch her push more sand into the middle. I copy

her, spreading my fingers wide against the cold sand. It's soft, unlike the sand in my backyard.

Together, we pile the sand as high as we can. Jenny steps back and examines it, her tongue poking out of her mouth.

"We need a flag." She takes a look around and takes off for the back part of her yard. Our other neighbor has plants growing along the fence.

"Wait! Jenny!"

She cries out after grabbing the cactus's leaf. Holding her hand, she stomps her foot, tears streaming down her face.

"Mommyyy!"

I rush to her, sliding to a stop. "Ssh. Ssh, Jenny. I'll get it out."

"Mommy!" She draws her hand away, sitting down on the ground.

"Let me get the poker out, Jenny."

She stops crying, letting out a small hiccup. Slowly, she holds her hand out, letting me see. One little poker from the cactus is sticking out of her finger. I take it and pull.

Jenny yelps, fresh tears forming.

I hear the back door open and the grown-ups are coming outside. Jenny's mommy is running across the yard. "What happened?"

Jenny cries, lifting her arms to her mommy, leaving me standing there with the cactus poker in my hand.

Miss Jackie hugs Jenny, telling her to calm down.

midnight**SHOW**

Mommy looks at me. "What happened?"

I hold up the poker. "She touched a cactus."

Mommy smiles at me, taking the poker. "You got it out? That was very sweet of you, baby." She messes my hair before tossing the poker back over the fence.

Jenny lets go of her mommy and points at me.

"He got it out, Mommy."

"He did?!"

She nods. "Yep. He wasn't even scared." She wipes her nose with her hand.

Miss Jackie smiles. "Brandon's your hero, isn't he?"

I feel my cheeks get hot and I look to the ground, kicking a rock.

Miss Jackie squats down, letting Jenny down next to me. Jenny's arms wrap around my neck, and she hugs me.

I return her hug, feeling happy.

"Come on, let's go inside and get you guys some juice." Miss Jackie pushes Jenny toward the house. Jenny's hand wraps around mine and she drags me along, our mommies behind us.

I hear my mommy giggle and whisper to Miss Jackie. "He was very close with the Valentines' little boy. Looks like he may have a little girl friend now."

57

SEVEN
Brandon

I watch the sweat drip slowly off my glass, the bourbon coursing through my body. Taking another sip, I swish the liquid around my mouth, allowing the burn to take over before swallowing. Setting the glass down on the table, I stare at the snow dancing around the television screen. I smile before standing up and turning off the white noise radiating throughout the house.

I need quiet to think.

Walking into the kitchen, I grab the bottle of Jim Beam off the kitchen counter where Jenny placed it this afternoon. I can still smell her, the scent driving my heart wild and my mouth water.

Michael walks in from the back room, carrying his shoes with him.

"You're just going to take a back seat to Ronnie, aren't you?" A creepy laugh echoes through my thoughts. Placing my head in my hands, I sway against the counter.

"It's just… how can she say she loves me yet not be here with me? How can she be out with someone else tonight?" I unscrew the top of the bottle and take a swig.

"It doesn't have to be this way, Brandon." Michael takes the bourbon from in front of me. "All the hurting can stop. You know this." He drinks from the bottle, handing it back to me.

Tears brim my eyes as I take another drink. For years, I've carried so much hate. For years, I've suffered in silence, Jenny being my only beacon of hope and love. But she's made it clear, she doesn't want me.

I never wanted it to be this way.

No one is going to save me now.

No one is going to stop me.

My mind clouds over as the room goes dark.

Tonight, she will know the mistake she's made.

EIGHT
Brandon

March 2014 - Age 21

I place my bowl of Ramen on the coffee table so I can settle into my futon. Turning on my second-hand television, I pick up my bowl, and slurp a fork full of noodles.

Happy birthday to me.

Three years ago tomorrow, the day after I turned eighteen, I moved into this small apartment built over a garage.

I snicker. Apartment is a far-fetched dream.

But this place was mine.

Mine to come and go as I pleased. To sleep through the night without my father waking me in a fit of random rage. To escape the memories of my mother that continued to line the walls.

My place to be free.

The television only picks up three channels, and I choose the least fuzzy version of Wheel of Fortune. Even after all these years, I never worried about upgrading. I'm content with the way things are.

Taking another bite, I watch the contestant spin the wheel, picking up her dollar tag.

Stuttering, the contestant calls out an 'g', flipping three tiles over. She jumps up in excitement.

Chill lady. You haven't won yet.

A flash of Jenny calling out the answers, bouncing on her living room floor comes to mind. She'd wait until the final tile was flipped before she'd jump up and do, what she would call, a victory dance. I would laugh at her and give her hell for being such a bookworm. Nine times out of ten, she'd stick her tongue out at me and call me a jerk, a wide smile on her face as she'd sit back down.

Those smarts are what got her into college.

What took her away from me.

"Brandon!" She yells into the phone. The receiver falls from my hand to the floor, making all sorts of racket. Dad is lying on the couch, snoring. Quickly, I grab the phone off the floor and hold my breath.

"What the hell, Jenny?" I whisper into the receiver.

"Sorry, come over! Mom's ordering pizza."

"Pizza? What's the occasion?"

"Just get over here."

Hanging up, I peer around the corner to see Dad still

passed out. Grabbing my backpack off the floor, I rush out the back door and across the yard to Jenny's house.

I always catch a case of butterflies as I walk into her house. Even though we just left each other, I already missed her, just like every time we're apart, which isn't often. She's the only reason I haven't left that house yet.

I step into her living room and can hear her and her mom laughing in the kitchen.

"Hello?" Rounding the corner, I see them each holding a glass_of what looks like champagne. Jenny picks up the third glass sitting on the counter and pushes it into my hands.

"Cheers!" She clinks our glasses and takes a long gulp.

Miss Jackie places her hand on her daughter's glass, slowing her down. "Careful, sweetie. Don't need you puking." She beams at me, clinking my glass as well. "Brandon, how was your day, dear?"

I sit back onto a bar stool and take a sip. "Not too bad." I eye the glasses. "So what's going on?"

Jenny waves a piece of paper in the air, thrusting it in my face. "I got in!"

"Stop moving so I can read the damn thing, goob." I chuckle as the words come into focus.

"Dear Miss Samms... You've been accepted... Full scholarship..."

I stop reading and look up at her slowly. "University of Southern California?"

She squeals, throwing her arms around me. "And a full scholarship too! Oh my gosh, Brandon! I'm going to college!"

I wrap my arms around her, holding her close, breathing

her in. Orange blossoms and sandalwood. It's from a perfume I gave her for Christmas. Tears pricked as I take a deep breath.

Jenny shifts to straighten up, and I quickly drop my head to hide my face.

Who knew a person could be so proud and so disappointed at the same time?

"Brandon? What's wrong?"

I knew I wouldn't be able to hide my sadness with Jenny. She knows me better than anyone.

I stand up, finishing my glass of champagne. "I gotta go."

Jenny's lower lip jutted out. "But, but you just got here." She points to her mom. "Pizza's coming and..."

I raise my hand to stop her. "I'll be back for that. I just need... I just need to take a walk." I kiss her forehead and push past her to the front door. Once it closes behind me, the tears spill over. My chest tightens with each step I take away from her place.

I can't... what am I going to do without her?

Oh relax, you want what's best for her, don't you?

But she's leaving! I have to tell her-

Pft. Like she's ever going to love you back.

Grabbing my head, I push on my temples, trying to make some sort of sense of the voices bickering.

I walk faster, as if my feet are trying to carry me away from everything behind me.

Ten minutes later, I turn the corner to start heading back. Despair and hopelessness cloud my mind, but I can't let her think I'm not happy for her. Brushing the last of my tears away, I glance at a small sign in someone's yard. It's a 'FOR RENT' *sign. In small print written in permanent marker, the sign states that there's a loft over the garage for rent. $300 a month.*

"Our way out." I mutter, before grabbing the sign from the yard.

Before I can talk myself out of it, I stroll up to the front door and knock. I have a little money saved up from my restaurant job, and I know I'll get more hours once school's out. I can live here. Get away from Dad. Start my own life and show Jenny that I can get it together.

Maybe she'll see the future I see.

An hour later, I'm walking back up her driveway. Jenny's sitting on the stoop, her head down on her knees.

"Hey."

She starts, looking up. I watch her face crumple as she pushes off the steps and into my arms.

"Brandon! I was so worried." She cries into my shoulder as the guilt of making her feel this terrible washes over me.

"I'm sorry, Jenny. I'm so proud of you." I push her off my shoulder and smile at her. I dip my head down to catch her eye. "Seriously. I knew my little Bookworm would do it."

She nods, hugging me around the waist. "I don't want to leave you."

"I know." I tuck her under my chin and let her warmth cloud my mind, suffocating the voices' grumblings.

Jenny sniffs before letting me go. "Come on. We still have to celebrate."

"Big news, right." We walk up the steps, Jenny still wrapped around me.

"Well that was just a side celebration." Her eyes twinkle

as she opens the front door. "The real celebration is you." I look into the living room to see streamers dangling down the wall and the smell of cake. "Happy Birthday, Brandon."

I blink, the television buzzing with snow. It's dark outside, and my bowl is overturned in my lap.

"Shit." I grumble, scooping any remaining noodles back in. My head starts to pound as I stand up, searching for a towel.

Just as I finish cleaning up the mess, there's a knock on my door.

9:42... Who could this be?

I peek through my curtains to see a police car in the driveway, my landlord outside watching my apartment.

What the-

They knock again. My stomach leaps into my throat as I pull on the knob.

"Brandon Fenwick?"

I nod, staring the cop down. He's a little taller than me. Looks young.

"Brandon, I'm Officer Mark Sampson. May I come in?" He takes his hat off, playing with the edge with his fingers.

"Am I in trouble?"

He stops fidgeting, shaking his head. "No. I just, well," he gulps and lets out a long breath. "Brandon, it's about your father, Jonathan Fenwick. He was in an accident."

Something cold washes over me, my blood turning icy before the warmth of joy and elation take over. I hide

my smile as I ask. "Did he-?" But I knew before Sampson said anything that Dad was dead.

The cop shakes his head again. "I'm sorry. He ran off the road. There was a semi in the next lane." Sampson's voice cracks as he runs his hand through his short hair, tugging at his neck. I can tell this may be his first time having to deliver this kind of news. I feel for the guy.

I swallow. "Is there anything I have to do?"

Sampson holds his hand up. "No. Um, the body is being moved to the Mountain View Hospital down the road." He shifts, turning back to his partner behind him. "Do you want me to take you?"

I shrug. "Nah. That's alright. Thank you." I close the door and walk into my make-shift kitchen.

I hear another knock and I sigh. Stupid cop.

Before I can even get the door opened, Michael is bursting through, helping himself to my couch.

"Hey man! What did you do?"

"Do?"

He juts a thumb towards the door. "Cops. What were they doing up here?"

"Came to tell me Dad died."

"He's dead?"

"Yep."

He lets out a whistle. "What now?"

"Hmm." I grab a beer from the mini fridge and crack it open. Leaning against the counter, I ponder that question. "I guess I can move back into the house. Get rid of everything before selling it." I take a long pull from the coldish beer. Fucking mini fridge doesn't seem to be working.

My fist closes tightly around the can, crushing it slightly before heaving the can across the room, spraying beer everywhere. A strangled cry falls from my throat as I collapse to the floor. "Don't make me go back there!"

Time to face the truth, Brandon. Time to go back. You're all alone now.

"No!" I cry, pounding the floor with my fist. "That's not true."

"What would you call it? Face it. You need me."

"I never said I didn't." I whimper, curling into myself.

There's another knock on the door, but I don't have the strength to push myself up. I look up for Michael's help, but he's nowhere to be seen. Probably panicked over my little episode.

"Ssh, there, there. I'll take care of this. Get up."

The room seems to move in slow motion as I make my way to the door. The lack of control feels... relieving. Like I'm watching a television show about someone else's life. Not my shitty one.

I watch my hand open the door, my dirty landlord standing on my stoop. "What were the cops doing here, Brandon?" I can see the powder dusted under his nose. His thin body barely covered by filthy clothes.

"Don't worry, Larry. They were just letting me know my dad is dead." The nonchalant attitude my TV-self is spewing is incredible.

"Oh." Larry scratches his forearm. "Listen, I can't have cops snooping around. You need to get out of here."

I feel my face fall, the voice in my head cursing. "Are you fucking serious? You're kicking me out?!"

Larry shrugs. "You understand." He sniffs, rubbing his nose.

"Yeah," my voice is suddenly deeper, gruff and angry. "I understand. I understand you're an asshole."

Larry backs up a step, his jaw dropping. "It's nothing personal-"

I take a deep breath, filling my lungs. "Oh, well that makes it better." I sneer, my chest puffing, heart beating in my ears. "Don't worry. I'll be gone soon enough."

Larry takes another step back as his eyes growing wide. His arms swing violently as he tumbles back down the stairs. I can hear the gruff voice laugh as I watch my hands slam the door shut.

Grabbing a bag from the closet next to the door, I pack it with all the stuff I brought with me – some pants, a few shirts and my jacket – and throw open the door.

Larry is still on the ground as I trot down the steps. As I get closer, I notice blood pooling around his head. "Brandon." He chokes. "I need help."

"Name's not Brandon." I reach into his pants pocket, pulling out his cell phone. Dialing 911, I toss the phone onto his stomach. "Thanks for housing the kid."

The street starts to fade to black as I walk towards my old home.

NINE
Brandon

Age 21

The sun is streaming in as I blink awake. Sitting up, my heart leaps into my throat.

I'm in my old room.

Surrounded by the things I left behind.

My ears strain for any noise, but no one is home. Slowly, my foot hits the floor, my hands grasping the blanket.

Why am I here?

"Your dad's dead, remember?"

Blanket falling from my hands, I cradle my head, trying to remember the events of last night.

"Last night? Pft. That was three days ago."

Three days? A wave of nausea hits my stomach. Have

I been asleep this whole time?

"Don't worry. I got it under control."

The sound of a closing door turns that wave into a full blown tsunami. He's here. He's not dead...

"Brandon?"

A woman's voice floats through the halls and I immediately relax.

My Jenny.

Pushing off the bed, I bolt for the living room.

She's here.

She'll make it all okay. I haven't seen her since her Christmas break two months ago but it feels like a lifetime.

Skidding to a stop, I drink in the sight of her. Dressed in a simple black dress and flats, her blonde hair pulled back in a ponytail, Jenny is moving some pillows around, cleaning up the remains of an old pizza box from the coffee table.

As she straightens up, she catches my eye. She gives me a small smile, puts the box down and walks straight into my arms.

"I'm so sorry, Brandon." She whispers into my chest. I choke back a sob, running my hand over her hair. I take a deep breath. Same hints of orange blossoms and sandalwood as before.

She pulls back, dabbing her eyes with her fingers. "Are you okay?"

I take her hand, holding it against my chest. "I'm better than okay. Now."

A blush crosses her face and she looks down, pulling her hand slowly away. "Come on. You need to eat some breakfast and get dressed. I have a suit for you."

"A suit? For what?"

Jenny's eyes widen. "For the funeral." A fresh set of tears brims her eyes as she bites her lip.

"Oh." I swallow and turn into the kitchen. The place is a wreck, and I can't remember if it was me who did this or the old man. Either way, I'm a bit embarrassed.

Jenny doesn't bat an eye and goes about pulling eggs from the fridge and bread from the cabinet.

"Um... come on. Throw some pants on. Mom'll make us something." She tosses the bread and eggs in the trash and washes her hands.

I look down. I didn't even realize I was still in boxers when I ran into the living room. Back in my room, I throw on what I had on the floor, running my fingers through my hair. I'll need to shower after I eat.

Jenny is waiting on the couch, looking around the room when I walk back in.

She's too beautiful to be in this dump.

Silently, we step into the sunlight and toward her house, our hands intertwined.

"Who else is here?" I point out the red sports car parked behind her mom's car.

Jenny's cheek flush, dropping my hand. "That – that's Ronnie."

"Who's Ronnie?"

Jenny's creaky screen door interrupts me as a guy

steps out of the house. He smiles and in two strides is standing in front of me. We're eye to eye as he jets his hand out. He's the rich, good-looking type. The kind of guy I have always loathed. Successful. Has their shit together.

I can't stand those types.

"Hey. You must be Brandon."

I take his hand, firmly, "You must be," I give Jenny a side glance, "Ronnie?"

Ronnie's smile tightens. "That's right. Sorry to hear about your dad, man. If there's anything I can do." Ronnie slaps his hand on my shoulder.

My eyes dart to his hand before I give him a cold smile. "Thanks."

A small hand falls onto my sleeve and I loosen up. Jenny gives me a look telling me to behave before she smiles, squeezing my arm. "Come on. Let's get that breakfast."

Ronnie stays at Jenny's as she and I walk back to mine.

"Good."

My conscience has been fighting me all morning. Thoughts of Jenny being with this guy ran over all logic, a deep voice screaming to confront her.

Whore! Slut! How could she?!

I sat there, ashamed at the words I was thinking.

I couldn't really feel like that, right?

Not about my Jenny.

Still, I couldn't help but listen to the cries from my mind. I feel betrayed and alone.

Doesn't she know?

"Get in the shower, Brandon. I'll get your suit ready."

"Where did you get me a suit?"

She ducks her head and pushes me toward the bathroom. "Go. We can't be late."

I swallow the lump forming in my throat and shut the door behind me.

"Why didn't you say something?" I whisper to the mirror.

"Because you're a pussy. Can't be tough like me, could you? I would do what needed to be done." The deep voice snorts. *"I wouldn't sit here quietly."*

Slamming my hands down on the sink, I shut my eyes, desperate to shut it up. "Leave me alone." I beg through clenched teeth.

"Fine." I can almost picture my old man throwing his hands up. *"Pussy."*

I hear a soft knock on the door. "Hey. You okay?"

"I'm fine." Pushing off the sink, I turn on the water and undress. My head hurts again, and I feel like I've been hit by a car.

I just need today to end.

I blink.

They're lowering his casket into the ground; a preacher muttering something I don't understand. Jenny and her mom are standing on each side of me, Miss Jackie wrapping her arm around my shoulder as Jenny holds my hand. Neither one are crying; just grave, solemn looks stretching across their faces.

The creaks of the lowering device stab my ears and suddenly, I can't breathe.

A small boy starts to cry, asking for his mommy.

A whiff of bourbon flutters by, followed by the harsh words of a drunk.

My body stiffens, my vision darkening around the edges. Knees buckling, I start to fall onto the ground, a strangled cry bellowing from my throat.

The last thing I remember is a pair of Spiderman shoes and the overwhelming feeling of despair.

TEN
Jenny

After the Funeral

I pace the living room, waiting for my mom to get Brandon to bed. Ronnie is sitting on the couch, watching me.

"Are you going to be okay?"

I stop biting my thumbnail, my eyes fixed down the hall. "I'm fine." My nail going right back into my mouth.

Ronnie stands up, his hand suddenly pulls my nail from my mouth, locking his gaze with mine. "No. You're not."

I drop my head. Bringing Ronnie was a bad idea. He doesn't need to see this side of my life. We've only dated for a few months; he's going to run after this. And Brandon's reaction wasn't what I expected. I should have known better.

"I'll *be* fine." I retort. "I'm just-"

Ronnie stops me. "I know. He'll be alright. This isn't an easy thing to go through."

I nod.

Brandon had been a stone wall throughout the entire service. It had been a small one; only a few of Brandon's dad's poker buddies came out, along with me and my mother. Ronnie came, but hung back out of respect.

It wasn't until they started to lower the casket did Brandon show any emotion. He completely broke down in front of me, something I didn't think he was even capable of doing. He fell so fast, Mom and I couldn't catch him in time.

And his cry.

I'll never forget that sound.

Ronnie stepped in and helped us get him to his feet. But when Brandon saw Ronnie, his eyes grew wide and he straightened up and stopped crying immediately. His hands grasped my arms, fear sweeping his tear stained face. I watched as the fear was suddenly replaced by something else, his body turning rigid.

Ronnie dropped his grasp from Brandon and took a step back, his hands up in surrender. Brandon sneered before shrugging me off, walking away.

Not five feet down the gravel walkway, Brandon collapsed.

I remember running to his side.

I remember the panic rushing though me as his eyes

stared blankly toward the horizon.

He slowly turned his head to me, a tear falling down the side.

"Jenny?" His voice was so small.

I cradled his head into my lap and kissed his forehead. "Ssh. Come on. I'm going to get you home now. You're okay."

But I don't believe that. Brandon's not okay.

The ride home, I sat in the back with him, his head on my shoulder. He would let out a child-like whimper every once in a while, but it would soon be followed up with harsh muttering. I couldn't make out the words, but I didn't try either.

I can't remember what exactly happened to his mom. I was a little kid. I just remember the funeral. Neither Brandon nor Mom will talk about what happened. She just always reminds me that we need to watch over him.

I know he hated his dad. I didn't like him either, and I told him to report the abuse every time there was a new bruise to cover up. But Brandon refused. Said there was no use. That no one is going to care enough to do anything. I finally stopped pushing it. I just kept watch like Mom told me to.

"We're all he has, Jenny."

She tried calling the cops one day, but Brandon snatched the phone from her, begging her not to. Their ten-minute fight ended abruptly when Brandon threw the phone across the room and into the wall.

He showed up the next day with a new phone and a

bucket of Spackle. Mom only smiled, offering him to stay for dinner.

The sound of a door shutting brings me out of my thoughts. Mom walks into the living room with a tight smile. "He'll be okay. I think it's shock."

I feel my face screw with anger. Shock? Is that what we're calling this?

"Mom. He needs help. We need to call someone."

Mom wrings her hands together as she steps into the kitchen. I follow her, watching her start to straighten up. She picks up a pile of dishes, taking them to the sink. She always cleans when she's nervous.

"Mom. You know I'm right."

She turns on the water, squeezing soap into the basin. I walk to her side. "It'll be what's best for him."

"Ms. Samms?" Ronnie's voice floats in from behind us. "I know some good doctors. I can call around for you."

I give him a weak smile before patting my mom's hand.

She sighs and shuts her eyes. "I just don't-he's never been one to ask for help. I know he'll be upset over this." Her lip quivers as she inhales. "He just lost his father. Of course, he's upset." Her eyes travel to the hall. "But if you think it's best, Jenny, then I'll help."

"Thanks Mom."

I hug her tightly before turning to the sound of what seems to be a crying child in Brandon's room.

ELEVEN
Brandon

My palms are sliding off the steering wheel as I sit outside the Inspire Theater. I wipe my hands nervously down my pants legs. It's so hot in here.

"You seem nervous." Michael chuckles as he lowers his head to stare out the windshield, across the street. Jenny is sitting on a bench outside the theater, playing on her phone. "She must be waiting on him."

I choke back my distaste at that idea as I study her.

I don't know if I've ever seen her look like this before. My eyes travel up her legs, and I lick my lips with desire. How come she never dressed like that for me; her skirt short, hair done in big curls?

"She's looking pretty good." Michael wipes a bead of

sweat from his top lip, running his hands through his hair. "Kinda whore-like, right?"

"Shut up."

Michael shrugs before opening his door. "You know what you need to do." His voice has dropped a bit, serious like. His eyes are wild, watching everything around us. He steps onto the sidewalk and slams the door shut, not another look back.

"I just need to talk to her." I mutter, shaking the loud cursing going on in my mind. I pull away from the curb and cross the street, parking in the loading zone in front of Jenny's bench.

I roll my window down, a slight breeze offering a touch of relief. "Hey."

Jenny jumps, frowns and stands up, her skirt hitching up just a little more. My pants pull uncomfortably at the idea of just what's under that skirt.

"Hey. What are you doing here?" She's leaning against the car, her low-cut top showing me things I have only imagined.

"Can we talk?"

"Now?" She looks behind her.

"Yeah. It'll only take a sec." I flash her a somewhat normal grin and I hear her sigh.

"Alright, but just for a sec, okay?" She pushes off the car, muttering, "He's late anyway."

"Get in. I'm holding up traffic." As she makes her way around the car, I call out, "Thank you," praying the shakiness I feel isn't in my voice.

She looks around once more before climbing in, her perfume taking over my car. My head spins with the lusty smell.

As I pull down the street, I watch her play with the hem of her shirt out of the corner of my eye, her hair hiding her face.

She's nervous.

"You look good."

"Thanks."

I take a deep breath. "I'd never be late for you."

She stills. "Are *you* serious right now?" She's biting back words but won't look up.

After a few more uncomfortable moments, I clear my throat. Jenny finally looks at me.

"Aren't you going to talk?"

Taking another deep breath, I open my mouth to speak. My tongue feels swollen and dry and the ability to find the words escapes me.

I can't do this.

Michael's voice booms in my ears, desperate. *"Tell her how much you need her! Tell her how she's saved you! Tell her the truth!"*

"Pussy." Another voice mutters. *"We don't have time for this."* My sight starts to grow dark. *"I'll take it from here."*

TWELVE
Jenny

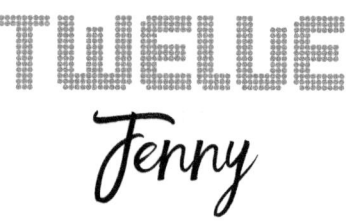

ell, Brandon. Talk." I can feel my patience waning. We've driven around the block at least five times, and he hasn't said much. I've said my apologies. Now it's his turn.

Looking out the window, I realize we're not on the same block.

Something's wrong.

"Um... Bra-"

He shoots me a sideways glance, sweat beading on his forehead. His tongue darts out to lick his lips.

Nerves flutter through my chest as I turn to him. "Brandon, you need to take me back."

Something's not right.

"Brandon's not here, sweetheart."

A shiver runs down my spine. That's not Brandon's voice. It's deeper, grave. It reminds me of someone...

"What did you just say?" I can barely hear my own voice.

The strange voice starts to laugh; a cold, dark laugh that causes my hair to stand on end.

"I said, Brandon's not here." He reaches across to the passenger side and takes my hand. It's rough and sweaty. Not at all like the hand I've held so many times before. "Relax, my Jenny. It won't be long now."

Slowly, I reach into my purse sitting between me and the car door. Running my fingers over the screen, I pray that I'm able to call someone. Anyone.

Maybe they can track me.

Please, Ronnie. Pick up.

Mom? Are you there?

As Brandon continues to drive, I search for anything to say to this impostor sitting next to me. I clear my throat.

Keep him busy.

Keep him talking.

"So, um, what's your name?"

He looks at me, his eyes traveling to my shirt. "Don't have one."

I pull on my shirt collar. "You don't have a name?"

In moments, we're pulling onto the highway, the city blurring past us. "Don't need one."

"How do you know me?"

The impostor snorts. "I've known you for as long as I've been around."

My blood runs cold. "And, how... how long have you been around?" I swallow, trying to make my voice a little less shaky.

"Ever since she died."

His face softens as he says this. He looks tired, his body slumping as he stares out through the windshield.

"Who died?"

"Mommy."

The voice coming from the driver's side is different now. Child-like and innocent. My hands start to shake as the little voice keeps talking.

"Mommy went to heaven. Daddy didn't like that. He would push me down and say mean things to me. But I had Michael to help me." The man looks at me. "And you." He gives me a smile that reaches all the way to his eyes.

A memory of that smile flashes through my mind. Brandon playing in my backyard. Running around, chasing me as we played tag.

Tears well in my eyes as I remember him. Before he was angry. Before he lost everything.

"I can still help you." I reach for his face, hoping to comfort him in some way.

Brandon's body shakes, a small whimper replaced by a gruff snort. My hand retreats.

"You had your chance. You can't help us anymore."

I glance out the window, Vegas slowly disappearing behind us. We haven't spoken since the child's voice told me his awful story. A local band is playing on the radio. I love this group. I remember dragging Brandon out to their shows a few years back. But I can't place the song, or the words. My mind is too busy trying to figure my way out.

After a few more songs play, Brandon pulls the car over, the city lights far off in the distance.

"Hey. Why did we stop?" My heart is pounding.

"There's a little place I want to show you." Brandon's face has softened, back to his friendly self. Back to the boy I grew up with. My best friend.

I try to swallow the nausea that is churning in my throat.

This isn't Brandon.

I look out the window, "I don't think we should go out there." I turn to face him, batting my eyes. "It's freezing. Plus, there's coyotes and--"

He takes my hand and kisses my knuckles. "Get out of the car, Jenny." His face twists with a cruel smile as he steps out of the car.

The sudden darkened car springs my brain into life, and I scramble to find the lock button on the door.

Too late.

The interior of the car lights up as Brandon pulls my door open for me, holding his hand out. His once beautiful, now manipulative smile, glowing in the moon light.

"Leave your purse. This will only take a minute."

Fighting back tears, I nod, fumbling into Brandon's awaiting arms. As the door shuts behind me, I hear a familiar chime from my phone. A tear falls as the phone continues to ring as we walk away.

"There, there, Jenny. This way."

Bile fills my mouth with each step away from the car. The lights from the city shining brightly from afar, like a haven. A light at the end of this dark tunnel.

"Where are we going?" I choke, tripping over my heels.

Brandon keeps his arm around my waist, holding me up while his other hand is clasped around my wrist. "It's a surprise." His smile is sickening as he gestures out. The moon is bright and I can make out a cluster of rocks. Something is laying on the ground beside them. As we get closer, I notice a backpack and a blanket.

Stopping in front of it, Brandon let's out a content sigh. "This is going to be prefect." He mumbles, pulling me to sit down.

My eyes dart around. Stretches of the Mojave Desert surround us, not a soul for miles. Sweat beads as I grasp for breath.

Brandon sits next to me, too close for it to feel normal. His hand still latched on to my wrist as he pulls a candle out of his bag.

"A little light to brighten the mood." The small flame dances as he stares at me. "We need to be together." His hand caresses my cheek. "I forgive you."

The gruffer voice is back, and Brandon looks like he's aged.

I swallow, my mouth dry.

No. This isn't Brandon. Not the Brandon I know. This

is a complete stranger, unhinged and terrifying.

The stranger chuckles, "This isn't right." He stands, dragging me along with him. Pulling me close, he starts to sway, humming gently to himself.

Fear finally lets me go and I search for whatever I can find to help me.

The stranger sets his chin on my head. "My Natalie. I'm sorry I got so mad."

I freeze. Natalie? Brandon's mom was named Natalie...

"Don't you forgive me?"

He stops his dance, glaring down at me. I swallow hard. "Yes. Of course."

His fingers cup my chin, lifting my face to his. "Then smile for me, baby. Like you mean it."

He smiles another sinister grin and leans down, kissing me. My stomach flips and I just stand there. I feel his hands slip from my waist to my lower back, his thumb running along the top of my skirt.

Panic grips me, my eyes flying open.

Off in the distance, I hear a semi horn.

My chance.

I slam my heel onto his foot, pushing him away from me. I start to run, kicking my shoes off.

The highway. It's right there.

Tears prick my eyes as I run, ignoring the rocks and plants cutting my bare feet.

I've got get to the road. It's my only chance.

I hear heavy foot steps behind me, and I will my legs

to move faster.

Just a few more steps. Keep going!

With a yelp, I fall to the ground, tackled from behind. I scream as I struggle to get out from under his weight.

But he pins me down, straddling me and holding my hands above my head.

"NO!" His voice rips through the night sky as the sound of the truck wizzes past us.

Something wet hits my cheek and I stop moving.

My best friend is sitting on top of me, crying. He's looks young again ashis head falling into my chest. His grip loosens from my hands, and he brings them to my side, hugging me as he cries.

"I can't. I can't anymore." He wails.

Slowly, I lower my hands to take his face.

"Brandon?" I whisper. I search his eyes. Maybe I can get him back. Maybe I can help him...

"You're the only one, Jenny. Nobody can help me like you. Please." He buries his face into my shoulder, sobs racking his body. "Help me."

I rub his back, trying to find the words to comfort him. "We can get you help, Brandon. Come on. We can get it right now." Slowly, I push myself up to try and sit. "We just need to go home."

"No!" Brandon straightens up, his face bitter. He pushes me back down, his fingers trace my body up, slowly closing around my neck.

"I can't forgive you, Natalie."

My heart pounds as the pressure deepens. I kick my

feet, trying to buck him off but his grip continues to tighten.

The eyes of my best friend in the face of this psycho gleam in the moon light, a sick smile twisted on Brandon's once soft face.

"I love you, Jenny." His words are a whisper as the sound of blood rushing pools in my ears.

Darkness creeps in the corners of my eyes as my lungs start to burn. A weird high I've never experienced takes over, as any air left in my body leaves.

Ronnie!

My arms and legs grow heavy, and my body slowly stops fighting.

Mom!

A sea of stars are the last thing I see before closing my eyes.

Brandon!

THiRTEEN
Brandon

"What did you do?"

"What needed to be done." He says in a strained, panicked voice.

I watch as my hands dig through the dried dirt of the desert, while a child cries softly somewhere close by.

"I don't understand."

I'm walking to my car, grabbing a shovel from the trunk.

"We can move on now, Brandon. No need to waste our lives on her anymore."

I'm running back into the desert, and I can hear him muttering.

Michael runs up beside me, his face white. "We gotta get out of here."

The moon has gone behind a cloud, hiding the path back to where I was digging. He spits out a curse as my feet trip over something on the ground.

Sprawled on the ground, I reach up to grab the shovel in front of me. I twist my body to see what I tripped on and look behind me.

The cloud moves out of the way of the moon as blonde curls come into view, the unseeing eyes of Jenny staring at me.

Jenny.

My Jenny.

"No." My hands want to cover my eyes and shield me from what I just saw, but *he* uses them to stab the ground with the shovel.

An agonizing scream bounces off the walls in my mind as I watch him and Michael bury her. I claw and fight, trying to stop him but *he* won't let me.

"Stop fighting, Brandon." Michael growls. "I need to fix this." He uses the shovel to tap the dirt down.

"Fix what?" I yell, my body wanting to cry. "Why did you do this?!"

"I didn't!" Michael screams, "But I'm tryin' to fix it, now shut the hell up!"

Sweat falls from my forehead as my hands finish the task at hand.

Slowly, darkness creeps in and my eyes close.

"Kill me. Please. Kill me now."

"No. Brandon, everything will be alright. I got this." Michael's voice is uncertain as he fades into the background.

Sobbing, I allow my mind to shut and I fall deeper into the despair that is taking over.

FOURTEEN
Brandon

My eyes peel open.

The living room is dark, and my head is throbbing. I slowly reach for the coffee table to find my phone, and my hand lands on a pill bottle.

Fuck.

Sitting up, resting my hand on my forehead, I blink to clear the fog from my vision. My Vicodin is sprawled across the table. The handle of bourbon Jenny gave me is almost empty next to it.

What did I do this time?

I cough, the taste of dirt filling my mouth. Rubbing my face, I stand up, stretching.

I feel like I've been hit by a damn truck.

My phone is sitting on a side table, dead. I plug it in

before making my way to the bathroom.

Fuck my life, I look like hell.

Dark circles line my very puffy eyes. Red dirt is covering my shirt. Confused, I look down. I'm still in my jeans, that are also dirty.

I look down to my hands. More red dirt cakes under my nails and small cuts are everywhere. I let out a breath and pull my shirt over my head.

I need a shower.

Standing under the hot water, I rack my memories for what happened last night.

A flash of Jenny comes to mind and my face falls.

I'm a joke. How can I prove to her we'd be perfect together if I'm always a drunken idiot? I must have gotten blacked out drunk and fell in my yard. Which explains the dirt.

Although, we don't have red dirt...

I let the water run cold before getting out. My mind doesn't seem to have much to say. Maybe I finally drank all the thoughts away.

Climbing out, I wrap the towel tight around my waist. I pick up the dirty clothes and dump them in my hamper. I'll do laundry later.

Finally dressed, my headache dropping to a dull throb. Back in the living room, I scoop the leftover pills back into their bottle and grab the bourbon. My fingers play with the yellow ribbon.

Jenny is like the color yellow – cheer and hope radiating off her.

And I fucked it all up.

Yellow is the color of friendship too. I remember her yellow dress the day we met. She was always supposed to be my best friend. I knew it the moment she crashed through the door to my house on a mission to get my mother's cookies.

I've been more than a terrible friend, and she deserves so much more.

A weight of guilt pushes me onto the couch and I reach for my phone.

Turning it on, I scroll through my texts for any hints to last night.

I see a missed call from Jenny, but that was two nights ago.

Two nights? The only time we didn't talk every day was when she went off to college. But there's not even a text from her.

I really screwed up this time.

I shoot her a text.

Me: I'm sorry.

That's all I can say to her. Nothing else matters. I have no excuse for... whatever it is I did.

I pull the curtains off to the side, checking for her car. Instead, I see a cop car where hers should be.

My heart leaps into my throat.

Jenny.

Michael rushes into the room, shutting the curtains closed. "Don't say anything. I'll take care of this."

I push him away and run out the door. He doesn't

follow.

Miss Jackie is standing on her stoop, hugging herself.

"Miss Jackie!" I push past the police standing on the steps and wrap my arms around her. She breaks down into my shirt.

"Miss Jackie? What's wrong?"

She cries harder, gripping my shirt. I rub her head, finally turning to look at the cops.

"Brandon Fenwick. I live next door."

The screeching of tires in front of the house pulls my attention away from the police. Ronnie slams his car door shut and beelines it for me. I push Miss Jackie around to stand behind me as Ronnie grabs my shirt, pushing me into the door frame.

"Where is she?!" Ronnie's eyes are blood shot.

I shove him off me. "What the fuck are you talking about?"

"Don't play stupid! You did this!" Ronnie pulls his arm back to hit me when the cops finally step in, pulling him away.

"Jenny."

I whirl back to Miss Jackie. She's barely whispering. She's not crying anymore, but she's on the edge. "Jenny is missing."

Jenny. My Jenny.

I have to find her.

"What do you mean?"

Miss Jackie looks up at me, almost like she's noticing me for the first time.

"Jenny was meeting me for a date." Ronnie chokes on his words. "She wasn't at the theater when I got there. And she didn't answer her phone." He rolls his shoulders out from the cops' grip. Digging into his pocket, he draws out his phone. "I did get an interesting message from her."

He pushes a button and a voice mail box recording comes over the speaker followed by muffled talking. Like when someone dials on accident when they sit on their phone.

Straining, I pick up a hint of Jenny's voice.

"I don't have-"

"You don't have a na-"

"-since I've been around."

That last voice. It's a man's voice. A familiar voice...

I step away from the phone, sweat beading on my forehead. "Who the fuck was that?"

"I don't know, Brandon. You tell me." Ronnie hands his phone to the police. "Here. Use it for evidence."

I look at Miss Jackie, her wide eyes still fixed on the phone. I take her shoulders. "I'm going to go find her." I kiss her forehead and back down the steps.

Ronnie catches my arm as I push past him. "Who is that Brandon?"

"How should I know?"

"*Stop talking!*" Michael's voice rings in my ears.

My eyes dart to the cops. "I don't fucking have time for this. I need to find her!"

Ronnie clenches his jaw. "It was you." He growls.

"What?"

Ronnie's grip tightens. "People saw her get into an old black mustang." He points to my car, its tires red with desert clay. My stomach lurches.

"You can't be fucking serious."

Ronnie's tongue darts out, licking his lips like a crazed man, his eyes wide. "I bet her phone's in there."

He lets me go, rushing to my car. I chase after him, shoving him from behind. "Touch my car and I'll kill you."

Ronnie falls on to my passenger side but doesn't turn to me. He pulls on the car door handle, flinging it open. He dives in as I grab him, pulling him out of my car. The cops have my shoulders, pulling on me. I let go of Ronnie and back away as they get a hold of him. As he climbs out, he holds something up in triumph, a crazed still look in his eyes.

Jenny's phone.

"Keep quiet." Michael says.

The police glance at each other before taking a hold of me. They slam me up against my car. I don't say anything.

"Brandon Fenwick, you have the right to remain silent..."

FIFTEEN
Brandon

The look on Miss Jackie's face haunts me as I ride in the back of the cop car. Her eyes burning with questions, disbelief and sadness.

Don't they understand? I love Jenny. Why would I hurt her?

"I'll tell you what to say when we get to the station." I turn to see Michael sitting next to me. His head is in his hand, leaning against the window.

"Station? I don't understand."

"Dude, shut up. Seriously, I need to think."

I shake my head, staring at the floor board. Michael has been repeating himself ever since I was placed in the car. I don't even remember when they took him.

"How come you don't have cuffs?"

Michael ignores my questions. "Okay, just so we're clear--"

"Let me go!" I kick the back of the cops' seats. "I need to find her!" Tears stream down my face as I picture my Jenny, lost and alone. My hands wring behind my back.

"Brandon! Knock it off!" Michael yells, spitting curses at me.

"Shut up!"

I shake my head furiously. "This is your fault!"

"I didn't do it! *He* did!"

"Hey! Chill out, pal!" The cop in the passenger seat slams his fist into the protective shield between the front and back seats. I give into my grief and continue to cry. The cop looks at his partner, his eyebrows raised.

I don't care. I don't give a damn what they think of me.

Flashes of the night my mom died come to mind and I feel myself fall, deeper into myself.

"Mommy?"

A small, sad voice starts crying and I can feel my body start to relax. I lay my head down in the seat next to me, now that Michael left, and curl my knees into my chest.

"I miss her too." I whisper, before closing my eyes.

I can feel hands pulling me upright. Voices and phones surround me as I start to wake up, my legs moving without my knowing. Once the fog clears, the police station comes into focus. I struggle for a second before remembering why I'm here.

Jenny's missing, and they suspect me.

Dropping my head, they lead me to the back. Without a word, I let them print me and take my picture.

I don't know where Michael is, and I don't hear the little boy crying anymore. That's just fine. I need to think clearly.

Leading me into a small room, they sit me down in a metal chair, re-cuffing my hands to be in front of me.

"Mr. Fenwick. Detective Sampson will be with you soon." And with that, the officer leaves me.

"Are you done with your little tantrum?"

I glare at the table. "Yes."

"Good. Now, get a hold of yourself. We can still get out of this."

The sound of a kid crying starts up again.

"Jesus... with this shit." A gruff voice mutters. I can almost picture him rubbing his temple, like my dad did when I annoyed him.

"Brandon Fenwick?"

I look up from the table. A man in a button-down shirt and tie is holding a file in his hand. His sleeves are rolled up to his elbows and I scoff. This guy looks like he just walked off the set of NCIS. Lame.

"I'm Detective Mark Sampson. I just have a few questions about Jenny Samms." He pulls out the chair in front of me. "First things first. Do you have a lawyer you can call?"

"No." I clench my jaw. "I don't need a damn lawyer. This is a waste of time."

"*Get a lawyer, Brandon.*"

The detective narrows his eyes. "Brandon Fenwick?" He mutters my name as he flips through his paperwork. "Didn't you lose your dad a few years ago?"

"Yeah."

"Lived in the backyard of a Larry Needlemen?"

"So? I had nothing to do with his coke problem."

Detective Sampson grimaces. "No. I, uh. I'm the one who came by your house that night."

I lean back in my chair. "Oh. Well, nice to see you again, Mark. How's life?"

Mark loosens his tie, running his hand through his hair. "It's good, Brandon. And yes, please, call me Mark."

"Great. It's like we're best friends."

"Exactly like best friends." Mark mirrors me, leaning back in his chair. "So, tell me, best friend. What's going on?"

I shrug. "Right now, my time is being wasted. I need to find Jenny, and you assholes won't let me go."

"We assholes are looking for her too." Mark takes a paper from the file. "Says here you may have been the last one to see her."

"Yeah, yesterday. She came by my house. We had a fight a few nights back and she came over to apologize."

"A fight? About what?"

I shift. "Nothing."

"Hmm." Mark looks at me, his fingers knitted under his chin. "Brandon, what day is it?"

I scratch my head. "Sunday?"

One of Mark's fingers run along his bottom lip. "Nope. Jenny has been missing since Saturday night. It's now Monday."

Red flashes through the room. "Then why am I here?"

"Because she was last seen with you, and her phone was found in your car. What's up with that?"

I shrug again, staring at the table. "I don't know how that got there." I whisper, playing with my fingernail.

"This isn't working." Michael's voice sounds tired. *"Get a lawyer, Brandon."*

I start to shake my head. "I love her. I would never hurt her." My voice sounds small. "Jenny's my best friend."

I look up and watch Mark's face fall in disbelief as my vision darkens again. I don't fight it, I just let my body sag.

"Brandon wouldn't hurt her." My voice changes from child-like to hard. "He's done talkin'. We need that lawyer."

I blink, hearing voices just outside the room. My head is heavy, my chest in pain.

"I want to go home."

Michael soothes. "I know. Soon. They're letting us go."

I hear the creaking of the door to the room and the therapist Jenny made me go see, Dr. Harrison, walks in, with a balding man behind him.

"Brandon? Are you okay?"

I nod. "Yeah. What's happening?"

Dr. Harrison sits in front of me, the balding man following suit. "Brandon, this is Mr. Phil Knowles. He's going to be representing you." The balding man reaches across the table to shake my hand.

Dr. Harrison takes a deep breath. "Brandon. It seems as though you've had an... episode. We've posted bail on your behalf so that you can go home." He lifts his hand up. "However, you need to make sure you stay in town."

I nod.

Knowles clears his throat. "Brandon, I want you to understand the severity of this. You are being accused of the disappearance of Jenny Samms. I'm going to talk to Dr. Harrison about your visits to him to help build your case." He slips a form from his breast pocket. "I just need you to fill this out to release your medical records."

"Why would you need these?" I scan through the paperwork. "What does one have to do with the other?"

Both men give each other a look. "Brandon, one of your alters may have done something with Jenny." Dr. Harrison shifts closer to me. "We're going to help them see that it wasn't you. You didn't harm her, at least not in the right state of mind."

My hands tremble as I finish my signature. I slam the pen down, my palms hitting the table top, my chair screeching as I jump from my seat. "I didn't harm her at all!" My voice is deep and gravelly again.

Dr. Harrison doesn't flinch but stands up to stare me down. "Sit down. I'm talking to Brandon."

"No. Brandon can't deal with this." Michael's voice travels from my throat. "Do your job, Doc, and get us out of this."

I lower myself back into my seat, the whimpering of a child coming to the surface.

My head hangs in my hands. "I swear to fucking Christ, this kid needs to shut up." I face the lawyer. "Do what you need to do. Brandon will work with you. We're done here."

And the room falls into blackness.

SIXTEEN

You did this, didn't you?

His heavy grunt is followed by a loud sigh. "Yeah."

My mouth shuts and I look at my hands. Swallowing, I nod. "Why?"

"She was cheating. Just like your mother." I can hear him shift. "Michael didn't want you to go through that."

I sniff, kicking at a dark background. There's nothing here. Just... emptiness. I can hear Michael talking to the doctor and my newly appointed lawyer. The kid has finally stopped crying. In fact, I don't even know if he's here anymore.

She's gone.

I know this.

I can't fight that anymore.

They, Michael and this other guy, won't let me tell the

truth. "Who's going to believe you?" Is Michael's only argument. He seems to be losing whatever control he may have had.

"She never cheated." I mutter. "She was never mine."

"That's not the point, is it?" I can hear his voice growing louder, like he's leaning in. "Why am I here?"

I shrug. "I don't even know you."

He chuckles. "Yes. You do. You know all of us. And we know you. The four of us have been here since the beginning."

"Four?"

"You, me, the kid and that guy out there, trying to keep your ass from the slammer."

I gulp, my stomach in knots. "But... but I didn't kill her."

He snorts. "Where am I, Brandon?"

I look around at the darkness, dread sinking in slowly.

My hands. He used my hands to do it. He used my face, my voice, my love for Jenny to kill her.

He clears his throat. "You needed to be rid of her. You'll thank me."

My hands reach for my hair, agony trembling through my body.

"Yes, thank you. I'll see you first thing in the morning."

I hear Michael talking to the lawyer. I watch as he shakes my hand, a grim and guarded smile on his face.

I'm leaving. I get to go home.

But what home? What do I have here? Nothing. My best friend's gone, never mind the fact that I live next to her childhood home. A home we played in. Laughed in. Cried in.

My legs start to move, and the police remove the cuffs. Detective Mark watches me, grasping my file in his hands. A look of remorse crosses his face as he turns to walk away.

I attempt to shake myself 'awake', to come clean as I'm walking out. But the others, they're keeping me in my place.

"You can break when we get away from here." Michael whispers.

The warm Vegas air is a beautiful change from the frigid police station.

Michael shields my eyes from the sun as my feet bound down the front steps. Once my eyes adjust, I see Miss Jackie and Ronnie talking to the detective. The same arms that held my Jenny are now comforting her mother. It makes my stomach turn and a growl slip from my lips.

A flash of Jenny's beautiful, cherub face, framed by matted curls comes to my mind. She's beneath me, her face dirty and streaked with tears. She's staring up at me, scared. I remember this moment. A brief time when I got away from the darkness in my mind and came to.

And she embraced me, welcomed me into her arms as I cried on her chest. She understood the pain I was in. She was going to forgive me.

Then the blackness came again.

Miss Jackie catches my eye as I walk away from them. I don't stop but we continue to stare for what feels like days. Finally, I break contact and duck my head. Stealing a glance, I see her jaw fall slack, her hand covering her mouth.

"She knows..." He growls.

Miss Jackie pulls away from Ronnie; heading in my direction.

I turn my back to her, look to the sky and keep walking.

"I bet it's my Jenny who's making this sky so blue." His voice is loving and tender.

He makes me sick.

"Not your Jenny. My Jenny."

If I could surface before, I can do it now.

A strangled cry pours from my throat as I fight to make myself heard. I feel my body fall, mid step, my head pounding.

Feeling like I'm back in my body, I cry out as all the voices fight to pull me back in.

"You fool!"

"No! What are you doing?!"

I see Miss Jackie run toward me, dropping beside me on the sidewalk.

"Brandon?"

"I did it." I whisper through clenched teeth. Her eyes grow wide as sweat breaks out over my body. "I... did it."

I see my vision is fading.

They're trying to pull me back in.

"Get away." I growl, pushing her back, my feet struggling to listen to me or to them. Detective Mark and Ronnie are running up to her as the voices finally win and pull me in. I push myself off the ground as the two men tackle me, my hand reaching for Mark's holster.

The gruffer voice sneers and my lip curls.

I won't live like this.

My fingers close around the butt of the gun, and I wrestle it away from them.

The sound of a car back-firing bounces off the buildings as my face hits hard concrete. There are screams and shuffling as something warm and sticky trails around my fingers.

As the surrounding chaos starts to fade into the background, I see a hand touch mine.

My eyes travel up a blue-tinted arm to locks of yellow hair.

Jenny.

I smile, ignoring the cries disappearing from my mind. "I think... I think the voices are gone." I croak.

She doesn't speak, but smiles warmly at me, nodding. The tint of her skin hides the bruising around her neck. Her hand cups my cheek, and I feel my soul pulling toward it.

She's here to carry me home.

With her.

Where I've always belonged.

EPILOGUE
Jackie

I didn't scream when Brandon shot himself.

I remember I was running toward him, trying to put all the pieces together when he fell.

He did it. He told me. But the struggles he showed me as he confessed haunt me still.

His demons were fighting with him, trying to keep him quiet before he ran.

As soon as the echoes from the gun fire settled, I had my first out of body experience. My body walked to him, laying a hand on his. I guess I needed to see him, to see that he was gone for myself.

Brandon looked so peaceful. So happy. His eyes were fixed to the sky, a smile frozen on his blood-stained face. At that moment, I knew Jenny was dead too.

A few days later, her body was found, outside the city in the middle of the desert. They kept telling me that she was found in a peaceful manner, her clothes intact, no signs of trauma. Like they thought that would help me.

It didn't.

Ronnie and I were able to give her a proper funeral, full of flowers and memories. Her friends from college came to show me support, telling me how sorry they were for my loss. We retreated to Ronnie's house for the reception. We couldn't have it at mine. It was too painful.

I lost two children that day.

The decision to leave and go back to my family in Colorado was easy. Packing up my home was not. My eyes kept darting out the window, watching the police tape sway in the wind.

Days turned into weeks before I finally got everything done. Most of my possessions sold or given to Goodwill, the rest packed in a small moving pod, already on its way to Denver.

Ronnie offered to drive me to the airport, and I finally accepted. I know it's been hard for him too.

So now, I sit here on my front steps, waiting for Ronnie to come.

The air has a small nip to it as a few clouds start to roll in from the West.

I stretch my legs out in front of me, staring at the street.

My imagination sees Natalie die that night so many years ago.

It sees Brandon walking up my driveway with my new phone and a can of Spackle to fix my wall after our fight.

It sees Jenny holding his hand as she drags him up the stairs for dinner.

I turn my head to look at the dark house next to me. It was never a home, and I pray that I can forget all the times I didn't do anything about that man hurting his son in it.

But that's neither here nor there. I didn't do anything and that's that. I will live with that regret for the rest of my life.

I stand up as Ronnie's car pulls into the drive, turning to take one last look at my past life.

A cool rain drop hits my cheek, and I look to the sky and smile. For the first time since that day.

I push a strand of hair behind my ear and pick up my suitcase. Ronnie stops at my bottom step, taking it from me. I give him a small smile, and we hug before he helps me to his car.

The wind whips around me as I reach for the handle, carrying the sound of small children laughing to me. I look around but see no one around.

My eye catches a small sandbox propped against the side of the house.

Shaking my head, I climb in and fasten my seatbelt.

A little girl's giggle floods my mind, and my hand

flies up to my mouth as she speaks.

"Ssh. It's okay. We're with you."

THE END

ACKNOWLEDGEMENTS

So many people to thank for getting this book off the ground!

Thank you, Aubrey Potter, for your continued guidance and help. Letting me flood your email with random scenes when you had no idea what I was even doing.

Jen Wyk from JaVa Editing and Alexandria Bishop from AB Formatting for making this story shine!

My beta readers: Brandi, Allie, Zeia, Josh and Bree and my proofreader: Eli. You guys pushed my creativity to the limits to make this story perfect.

Josh, this idea came from us. Our mutual love of music and the stories the songs tell inspired me. Our countless talks about the fan theories surrounding the Murder Trilogy are some of my favorite memories from our own story. Thank you, from the bottom of my heart.

And finally, thank you to the Killers. This story is my dedication to their music and to their talent.

I own no rights to any song by the Killers. All songs were an inspiration for this story. If you haven't listened to the band, I highly suggest it!

www.ingramcontent.com/pod-product-compliance
Lightning Source LLC
Chambersburg PA
CBHW070630130626
46555CB00006B/2517